LIVING WITH
LEARNING
DISABILITIES

LIVING WITH
LEARNING
DISABILITIES
A Guide for Students

David E. Hall, M.D.

Lerner Publications Company
Minneapolis

Acknowledgments

I could not have written this book without the things I have learned from my patients. In addition, the writings of Dr. Melvin Levine, Dr. David Burns, and Dr. Aaron Beck have been of great value. I am grateful to Lerner Publications for encouraging me to write this book, and to LeeAnne Engfer for her thoughtful editing.

Copyright © 1993 by Lerner Publications Company

LIBRARY OF CONGRESS CATALOGING-IN-PUBLICATION DATA

Hall, David E., M.D.
    Living with learning disabilities : a guide for students / David E. Hall, M.D.
      p.   cm.
    Includes bibliographical references (p. 62) and index.
    Summary: Describes various learning disabilities, such as attention deficit disorder, fine motor problems, and difficulties with visual information, and offers positive advice on how to cope.
    ISBN 0-8225-0036-1
    1. Learning disabled children—United States—Juvenile literature. 2. Learning disabled children—Education—United States—Juvenile literature. 3. Learning disabilities—United States—Juvenile literature. [1. Learning disabilities.] I. Title.
LC4705.H35 1993
371.9—dc20
                                   92-46600
                                       CIP
                                       AC

Manufactured in the United States of America

2 3 4 5 6 7 – P/MA – 00 99 98 97 96 95

This book is dedicated to my wife, Michelle, my parents, Bryan and Mary, and to Cheryl, who first interested me in learning disabilities.

Contents

Introduction

The purpose of this book is to help you understand learning disabilities. Maybe you have heard the term but aren't sure what it means. Your parents and teachers have probably talked to each other about your learning disability. They might not have talked to you about it. That's too bad, because the person who most needs to understand learning disabilities is you!

Your parents and teachers don't mean to leave you out. They might not be sure themselves exactly what learning disabilities are, or how to explain them to you. Learning disabilities can be hard to understand.

I am a pediatrician, a medical doctor who specializes in treating children and teenagers. I have worked with lots of kids who have learning disabilities. There are many things I wanted to tell them, but I never seemed to find enough time. That's why I wrote this book.

If you have trouble reading this book, ask someone (your parents, for example) to read it to you. They'll probably learn something from it too. If it seems like too much to read at once, read it in small sections. Not all of the book will apply to you, but some of it will. Remember the things that seem most important to you.

As you go through school, you will probably find many people—parents, teachers, counselors—who want to help you. In the end, though, you are the one who decides how you do in school or at a job. It's not your learning disabilities that hold you back as much as how you feel about yourself. That's the main point of this book.

What Are Learning Disabilities?

In nearly every classroom, there are students who seem smart but have trouble learning certain things. These students come up with good ideas, or are good at lots of other things, but they just don't do well in school.

In the past, parents and teachers usually told these students their grades would improve if they just tried harder. This advice didn't work, because the students were already trying as hard as they could! No one understood why they had so much trouble. Many of these students gave up on themselves. They felt like they were dumb or stupid. Sometimes they decided they were failures because they couldn't do well in school.

Now we know that these students were not bad kids or dumb. They had learning disabilities. A person has a **learning disability** if he or she has problems learning something despite being taught well and trying hard to learn. A learning disability can be thought of as a "wiring problem" in the brain that makes learning certain skills very difficult.

A person with a learning disability is like a TV with a connection that doesn't work correctly. This TV gets some channels well but not others. On channel 13 the picture might be fuzzy, and on channel 5 the sound might be hard to understand. But if you turn to channel 2, the picture is great—maybe even better than on most TVs.

A person with a learning disability is not stupid or mentally retarded. A person with mental retardation has trouble learning in *all* areas. In contrast, a person with a learning disability is good at some things but not others, like an athlete who is good at baseball but not so good at basketball. He might even be the best baseball player on his team, but he's the last one picked for the basketball team.

Some conditions can keep a student from learning but are *not* learning disabilities. These include:

1. *Hearing problems.* If you can't hear what the teacher is saying, you can't learn.

2. *Vision problems.* If you can't see the blackboard or your books, you'll have trouble learning.

3. *Psychological problems.* Some students have a hard time in school because they're thinking about something else, such as their parents' divorce or an illness in the family.

4. *No opportunity to learn.* Students might have problems in school if no one at home ever gives them encouragement, or if they go to an inferior school where very little learning takes place (for example, a school with overcrowded classrooms, problems with violence or drugs, or no money for supplies). Kids who don't learn in this situation don't have learning disabilities; they just have never been given the opportunity to learn.

5. *Mental retardation.* Kids who are retarded are slow in all types of learning and do not have what doctors call learning disabilities.

Students with learning disabilities can see and hear normally; they have been given plenty of opportunities and encouragement to learn; they don't have psychological problems; and they are not mentally retarded. Nonetheless, they have trouble learning important skills at school.

How common are learning disabilities?

Learning disabilities are very common. In a group of 100 students, 3 to 15 of them will have learning disabilities. Among every 5 students with learning disabilities, on average 3 are boys and 2 are girls.

Many people with learning disabilities have had successful careers. Some examples include: Cher, the actor and singer; Greg Louganis, the Olympic diver; Nelson Rockefeller, former vice-president of the United States; Thomas Edison, the inventor of the light bulb and phonograph; Tom Cruise, the actor;

Jackie Stewart, the British race-car driver; and Hans Christian Andersen, the author. And these are just some who became famous!

What causes learning disabilities?

Some learning disabilities are inherited, the way eye color or hair color are. Many people with learning disabilities find that some of their relatives had similar problems.

On the other hand, many other people with learning disabilities discover no apparent cause for their problem. It's something that just happened—no one is sure why.

Sometimes exposure to harmful substances, or **toxins,** can cause learning disabilities. Lead is the most common toxin associated with learning disabilities. In older houses, especially those built before 1950, lead is an ingredient in the paint on the walls. Lead poisoning occurs when babies and small children eat chips of paint containing lead. Less severe lead poisoning can develop when children inhale dust from lead-based paint. (By the way, you can't get lead poisoning from the "lead" in a pencil. Pencil lead isn't really lead—it's carbon.)

Alcohol and cocaine are other harmful substances that can lead to learning disabilities. When a pregnant woman takes drugs, they affect the unborn child's brain and sometimes cause learning disabilities or more severe problems.

Some medical conditions, such as Fragile X syndrome, can cause learning problems. Being born prematurely (too early) is not a common cause of learning disabilities, however.

The brains of people with learning disabilities appear to have developed differently than those of people without learning disabilities. One way to look at learning disabilities is that they result from a brain that is just too specialized. For example, you might be an expert at taking items such as bicycles apart and putting them back together, but you have trouble reading. Both abilities require the use of your brain, but not being able to read is more likely to affect your schoolwork.

Everybody has strengths and weaknesses. Some people's weaknesses affect how they learn at school, and these students are diagnosed as having learning disabilities. Many people with learning disabilities accomplish a lot at school and in their lives by taking advantage of their strengths.

It's important to learn as much as you can about your own difficulties so you can find the best way to cope with them. Having problems with some tasks doesn't mean you will have trouble with everything. In fact, almost everyone has a learning problem of some sort. School success is important, but don't forget that success means more than just good grades.

Still, you will need to get through school one way or another to get ahead as an adult. It's important not to give up.

Types of Learning Disabilities

Your brain does many things. It stores information: it remembers pictures, words, sounds, feelings, and movements. It solves problems: how things are put together, how they work. Your brain tells your muscles how to move. It directs your fingers when you write a letter.

If your brain has trouble doing tasks that are important for success in school, you have a learning disability. Doctors group learning disabilities into categories according to which brain function causes the difficulty.

There are different types of learning disabilities. As you read through the descriptions that follow, see which ones fit you best. None of the descriptions is likely to fit you exactly. Many people have problems in more than one area.

Attention Deficit Hyperactivity Disorder

The most common condition that causes learning problems is **Attention Deficit Hyperactivity Disorder** (abbreviated ADHD). Many people don't think of ADHD as a learning disability by itself, because it often overlaps with other conditions. About 6 out of 10 people with ADHD have some other type of learning disability too.

People with ADHD have trouble concentrating. They just can't keep their mind on their work. This might not be a problem if the activity is exciting. For example, many people with ADHD can concentrate for hours on TV or computer games. It's only when they have to do something they find boring, such as sitting in class and listening to a teacher, that they lose interest.

Everyone has problems paying attention at times. People with Attention Deficit Hyperactivity Disorder, though, have more trouble than most. When the teacher is giving instructions for homework, students with ADHD might be looking out the window or at the pictures on the bulletin board. They might be thinking about what they will do when they get home.

Students with ADHD tend to be inconsistent in their work. One day they get an A on a test, and the next day they get a D. Or they might miss the easy question on a test and get the hard one right. This probably happens because they concentrate on the hard one but not on the easy one.

Many students with attention problems rush

through their tasks and do poorly as a result. They might be the first to finish a test, but they don't do well on it. They tend to make mistakes because they don't check their work. It's hard for these students to learn that being first isn't nearly as important as doing a good job.

Organization is difficult for students with ADHD. A student might lose track of papers and assignments. He might complete his homework but forget to bring it to class. Sometimes he loses his homework assignment or puts off doing a project until the last minute.

Many people with ADHD have sloppy handwriting. This might happen because they find it hard to pay attention to their writing.

Many students with ADHD are very active. Some people call them hyperactive or "hyper." Kids who are hyperactive find it very difficult to sit still for any length of time. Not everyone with ADHD is hyperactive, though. Many girls with ADHD are not hyperactive. When hyperactivity is not a prominent feature of the disability, it is called simply Attention Deficit Disorder (ADD).

Many people with ADHD are impulsive—they act first and think later. That is, when they get the urge or impulse to do something, they just do it. This can get them into a lot of trouble. For example, a student with ADHD might blurt out to the teacher, "Wow, Mr. Smith, you have the biggest ears I've ever seen!" The other kids in class might also notice that the teacher has big ears. They just wouldn't say it.

Kids who are impulsive have a hard time telling themselves to stop when they get the urge to do something, even if they know it will get them into trouble. Often they feel very bad afterward about what they did.

Attention Deficit Hyperactivity Disorder isn't all bad. People with ADHD are often very creative. They tend to come up with ideas that other people don't think of. They are often good at seeing the big picture. Many kids with ADHD have a lot of energy. They often appear to have good memories. But sometimes they remember the wrong things. For example, they might remember what clothes the teacher wore one day, but they forget what their math assignment was.

Language disorder

ADHD is the most common learning problem. The next most common learning disability is language disorder. Of every 10 students with learning disabilities, 3 to 7 of them have problems with language. Language, of course, is how we use words to communicate with each other. Language problems include problems with reading and writing. People who are dyslexic have a language disorder. **Dyslexia** refers to a difficulty with the ability to read.

Language is the skill that is most crucial for success in school. Students who have problems with language often end up feeling pretty stupid. If you have problems with language, it doesn't mean you aren't smart in other areas, though. And it doesn't mean you can't learn to use language well.

Some people with language disorder have trouble coming up with the right word for what they want to say. They can't think of the name for something, even though they know what it is. Eric had a language-based learning disability. If his teacher pointed to her eyebrow and asked Eric what it was, he couldn't think of the correct word. He would say, "The hairy thing above your eye." He talked slowly because he couldn't think of the right words.

Many people with language problems or dyslexia find it very hard to understand what they read. This disorder leads to problems in school, because almost all schoolwork involves reading. Anything that requires writing, like a book report, is also hard. People with language problems may have trouble with math, too, especially word problems.

Some kids with language problems are shy, because they have a hard time thinking of the right thing to say. They might feel unpopular because they can't use words in clever ways that make other kids laugh.

Sometimes students with language disabilities get confused by words that sound alike, such as "hall" and "howl," or "shark" and "sharp."

Our brains are divided into two halves, called hemispheres. Scientists have discovered that the left side of the brain is used for most aspects of language, while the right side of the brain is used to deal with visual information. The right side of your brain deals with things like artistic ability, colors, and how things fit together.

People with language problems seem to have a problem with the left side of their brain. On the other hand, the right side of their brain often works very well or even better than average. So people with language problems might be very good in art or at building things.

Problems with finger coordination (fine motor problems)

Typically 1 to 5 out of every 10 people with learning disabilities have problems with finger coordination. You may hear teachers talk about "fine motor skills." **Fine motor skills** refer to a person's ability to control his or her finger movements.

Students with this problem tend to have sloppy handwriting unless they write very slowly. Fine motor problems may make it difficult to use scissors or tie shoes. Interestingly, some people with fine motor problems are very good artists. If your handwriting is poor, it doesn't necessarily mean that you will be weak in art. Most people draw pictures slowly and with a lot of care. Writing is much more automatic and is usually done very rapidly.

Fine motor weaknesses cause more problems as the amount of written material you are expected to produce goes up. Many people find it hard to communicate their ideas and write neatly at the same time. If you have finger coordination problems, you might find it easier to type. If you learn to type, then you can use a typewriter or computer.

Sometimes people with fine motor problems also have difficulty with tongue coordination. This condition makes it hard to pronounce words clearly. These students may need extra help in school from a speech therapist.

People with fine motor problems understand what they read, and they are often very intelligent. But because putting their thoughts on paper takes so much effort, they do worse in school than expected.

Sequencing problems and memory problems

A disability involving **sequence** makes it hard to do things in order or in steps. A sequence of numbers is "1, 2, 3, 4." A sequence of instructions is, "Take the math book off the shelf, get out a piece of paper, write your name at the top, then turn to page 14 and do the four problems at the top of the page."

If you have sequencing problems, you have difficulty remembering things you have to do in steps. For example, you might get lost after "turn to page 14." About 1 or 2 out of 10 students with learning disabilities have sequencing problems.

For some people, their difficulty with sequences stems from a memory problem. Others have trouble with sequences even though their memory is fine. They get the days of the week or the months of the year mixed up. Because of their confusion about time and dates, these students tend to be disorganized. They might have a hard time keeping their schedule of classes straight.

People with sequencing problems often have trouble memorizing phone numbers or addresses. They also may have problems with language, because forming sentences requires the use of words in a sequence. Sometimes their sentences are not easy for others to understand.

Some people have problems with sequences of things they see, some with sequences they hear, and some with both. Other people understand steps but can't keep them all in their mind at once. For these students, the problem is memory.

Scientists believe that there are at least two basic kinds of memory: long-term memory and short-term memory. Your **short-term memory** stores information that you need to remember only for a little while. For example, your teacher's instructions to get out your math book and turn to page 14 would go into your short-term memory. After you followed the instructions, you would not need that information anymore—you could forget it. If someone asked you a month later what page the math homework was on, you probably wouldn't remember. Your short-term memory keeps information for a short time while you need it.

Your brain stores information you remember on a more permanent basis in **long-term memory.** For example, your birthday, your address, and the color of your mother's hair are in long-term memory. Things in your short-term memory can be moved to long-term memory if you make a point of remembering them. Many students with learning disabilities have problems with short-term memory.

Problems with visual information

Some people are good at language but have problems understanding things they see. It's difficult for them to copy figures from the blackboard, and they may do poorly in art. Sometimes they have trouble learning the alphabet, because they don't recognize the shapes of the letters. They have no problem with talking and understanding what people say, though.

Doctors refer to this type of learning disability as a problem with **visual perceptual skills.** Just as the left side of the brain is more important for language, the right side of the brain is more important for understanding shapes and patterns and how things relate to each other in space. People with visual perceptual weaknesses may have a problem with the right side of their brain. Visual disabilities are not common. They account for school problems in only 1 learning-disabled student out of 10.

People with visual perceptual problems might not be able to tell left from right, especially in kindergarten or first grade. They often get letters mixed up. For example, they may confuse *b* and *d* or *p* and *q*. These students may have poor spelling, because they can't remember what the correctly spelled word looks like. In math, they don't line numbers in neat columns, so they add them up wrong. It's not that they don't know how to do the math problem, it's the way they put the problem on paper that causes the error.

Students with visual disabilities seem to lose things —keys, homework, jackets—because they can't remember where they put them. They tend to have messy desks. All these problems result from difficulty organizing things in space.

Testing for learning disabilities

When parents or teachers suspect that a student has a learning disability, they often send the student to a **psychologist** for testing. There are many kinds of psychologists. Some psychologists talk with people to help them deal with strong feelings of sadness or anger. Other psychologists try to figure out how the brain works and why people act the way they do. Others do tests to figure out why some students have problems in school.

If you have been told you have a learning disability, chances are you've been given some tests by a psychologist. These tests aren't like the ones you take in class. You don't pass or fail them. They are meant to help determine what you are having trouble with. For example, psychologists might test for language problems by asking you to name things in a picture, or to list particular items very quickly. You might be asked to name as many insects as you can in 60 seconds, for example. After you're tested, the psychologist will make a report about you, so your teachers can decide how to help you learn.

Your teachers and psychologists will probably talk to each other and to your parents about your test results, but they might not explain them to you. It is important that you understand your own strengths and weaknesses. Be sure to ask your parents, school counselor, or psychologist to explain your test results to you.

It can be very confusing to determine exactly what kind of weakness is causing school problems, because different types of disabilities can cause similar problems. That's why it's important to have a psychologist help you figure it out. Attention problems, for example, can resemble sequencing problems. If you don't pay attention to what the teacher or your parents say, you won't remember what you have to do, but it's not that you can't understand step-by-step instructions. Language problems might also result in some of the same weaknesses as sequencing problems.

What kinds of learning problems do you have, and what are your strengths?

Take some time to figure out your strengths and your weaknesses. Everyone has some of both. For example, I have problems with spatial relationships (my desk is always messy, and I can't remember where I put things) and with time (I often underestimate how much time something will take). My fine motor skills are not very good—my handwriting is sloppy. I also have had problems with organization, but this has improved as I've gotten older and learned how to organize my daily life.

On the other hand, I have strengths in figuring things out and understanding concepts (that is, the big picture—what things mean). I'm pretty good at language and at coming up with new ideas. People tell me that I am sensitive to their feelings.

What are you good at and not so good at?

There are many ways to be smart

Many kids with learning disabilities decide they are just dumb—and they give up. That couldn't be more wrong! There are many ways to be smart. School success is one way, but not the *only* way.

Another word for smart is "intelligent." One way people try to measure how smart you are is with an IQ test. IQ stands for "Intelligence Quotient." You may have heard people say things like "My IQ is 100," or "He has a high IQ." The number refers to the score someone gets on an IQ test. Psychologists created IQ tests in an attempt to measure intelligence.

Many people assume that students with high IQ scores are smart and those with low IQ scores are dumb. The fact is, IQ scores can be very misleading. One problem with IQ tests is that they only test *some* of your brain's abilities. If your strengths are in the abilities an IQ test measures, you'll probably get a high score. If your strengths lie in areas an IQ test does not measure, however, an IQ score will under-estimate your true abilities.

IQ tests are good for measuring some (not all) language skills, as well as problem-solving skills. There are many abilities and talents IQ tests *do not* measure very well or at all. For example:

Imagination and creativity
Musical ability
Ability to pay attention in class
Motivation—how much you want to succeed
Ability to work hard
Ability to tolerate frustration
How good you are at being sensitive to other
    people's feelings and getting along with others
Athletic ability
Ability to remember movements (this skill is
    important in dancing, for example)
Artistic ability
How good you are at building things

Your brain must work hard at these skills, but they are not measured well by an IQ score. Whatever your IQ score is, don't take it too seriously. (By the way, it is also possible to have a high IQ and still have severe learning disabilities.) Above all, don't conclude that you are stupid because of an IQ test.

Adjust Your Attitude!

The first and most important step in coping with learning disabilities—or any other problem—is to adjust your attitude.

Some students with learning disabilities give up. They decide that it's better not to try at all than to try and fail. They tell themselves that school isn't important and act like they don't care. They might say that students who do well are just "buttering up" the teacher. Your biggest enemy in school, though, isn't teachers, homework, your parents, or even your learning disability. It's two words: "I can't."

Attitude is what separates winners from losers—in sports, in school, and in life. Learning disabilities do not separate winners from losers. Many successful people have learning disabilities.

In sports, have you noticed that the home team

often has an advantage over the visiting team? One reason is that the players on the home team have the crowd cheering them on.

Have you ever done something wrong and had a friend say, "That's okay. You'll do better next time." Did it make you feel better? It's great when someone is cheering for you. There is one person who can support you and always be there when you need it— you! You can be your own cheerleader, even when things are going bad.

Suppose your best friend failed a test. Would you tell him he was stupid and a complete failure? Of course not. So why tell yourself that? You can be your own best friend. Learn to treat yourself kindly.

Most people are more critical of themselves than they would ever be of someone else. For example, some kids worry that if they do poorly in school, or have to go to a special class, no one will like them. But think about it—do you pick your friends based on their report card performance, or which class they're in?

The skills you need to get As in school aren't exactly the same as the ones you need to succeed in life. Good grades are important, but you're not a complete failure if you don't get good grades. You may have strengths that will be valued more in the adult world than in school. Whether you like it or not, however, you will have to get through school and pass your subjects. One thing that will help you succeed, in school or out, is a good attitude.

Stephen did very poorly in his classes in elementary school. His classmates laughed at him when he stumbled through reading lessons. They called him stupid behind his back, and he believed them. He lived in constant fear of failing a grade. He became convinced he would never achieve success in school or in a job.

Today Stephen is a doctor. What changed? His brain power was always there, but it was hidden by his learning disabilities. Stephen was tested by a psychologist who figured out that he had problems understanding visual information. Once Stephen understood why he had problems learning, he stopped telling himself he was stupid. Stephen changed the way he thought about himself. He needed some extra help unlocking the door to his brain power, but he was not dumb. He had to work harder on some things, and he made lots of mistakes, but he eventually mastered his school tasks. He didn't give up on himself.

Accepting a problem and turning it around to make something good out of it is one of the keys to success in anything. As the popular saying goes, "When life gives you lemons, make lemonade."

Mistakes are an opportunity to learn

Thomas Edison, the inventor of the light bulb (and a person with learning disabilities), made about 1,000 light bulbs before creating one that actually worked. A reporter asked him, "How did it feel to fail 1,000 times?" Edison replied, "I didn't fail 1,000 times. The light bulb was an invention with 1,000 steps."

If you don't make mistakes, you won't learn much. We all make mistakes. If Thomas Edison had called himself a failure after his 999th light bulb didn't work, you might be reading this book by candlelight. Successful people aren't much different from everyone else, except that they don't give up.

Jason hated to take tests. Whenever he missed a question, he told himself, "I'm a failure." He felt so bad about himself that his grades got worse and worse. Jeremy, on the other hand, didn't expect to be perfect. He knew he was going to make mistakes. Each time he told himself, "Good, I learned a lesson. Next time I'll know better." Both students had similar abilities. Which one do you think did better in school?

Can you learn to play baseball without missing the ball on a few swings? Can you learn to ride a bike without ever falling off? In the same way, you can't expect to learn much in school without making mistakes.

Lots of learning-disabled people give up. They're afraid of being embarrassed in front of their friends. They figure it's less embarrassing not to try at all. This may seem like a good idea at first, but it really doesn't work. It just gets you further behind. It doesn't fool anyone, either.

In many subjects, students are graded on class participation. Many students do not say anything in class, for fear of giving the wrong answer. Being quiet is not the best strategy, however. You'll do better if you say something. The teacher doesn't expect you to be perfect. In fact, teachers appreciate kids who are interested enough to say something in class.

It's also a good idea to admit your mistakes. Suppose your parents made a mistake and blamed you for breaking something your brother or sister broke. You would probably respect your parents more if they apologized to you than if they didn't admit their mistake because it might make them look bad.

People respect you more if you admit your mistakes. That includes your friends, teachers, and parents. Moreover, you can always turn your mistakes into something positive. You don't need to beat up on yourself because of a mistake. Instead, try saying to yourself, "I made a mistake. All people make mistakes. Good. I can learn something from it."

Thoughts that lead to failure

Earlier we discussed how students with learning disabilities sometimes come to the wrong conclusion about their abilities. They mistakenly conclude that facing difficulties in some areas means they will have difficulty in all things.

Many people make similar mistakes in deciding their worth as a person. They are much more critical of themselves than of anyone else. As a result, they end up feeling bad about themselves. The good news is that changing your thinking can make you feel better about yourself.

Get rid of the word "should" in your thoughts

Do you find yourself using words like "should" a lot? "I *should* know how to do this." "I *shouldn't* have made that mistake." "My parents *should* be on time to pick me up." "School *shouldn't* be so hard." "I *shouldn't* have to go to the tutor." "My parents *should* know I'm doing the best I can."

Of course, the word *should* is not always bad. It's okay to use it when you refer to laws of nature, for example. It's fine to say, "If I drop this rock, it should fall to the ground." On the other hand, if you apply *should* or *ought* to how things and people in the world affect you, it will do you absolutely no good. What it will do is make you feel bad.

People who use a lot of "should" statements end up feeling angry or guilty. They are unhappy much of the time, because they are constantly disappointed. Why? Because people don't act the way they "should," and things usually don't work out the way they "should."

Instead of telling yourself what you should do or how you should feel, try saying, "It might be nice if," or "I wish I could."

When you don't get something you expect or want, you probably feel angry. If you expect your parents to take you to a movie tonight, but they decide at the last minute not to go, there is a gap between what you expect and what you get, and it makes you angry. That's only natural.

If John expects to have a birthday party every day for a week, he will feel angry and disappointed six out of seven days. Whose fault is it that he is angry? His, or the people who don't celebrate his birthday every day? There's a gap between what John expects and what he gets. The problem is, he expects too much.

If your expectations about the way things should be are unrealistic, you'll just end up feeling bad. Get rid of the "shoulds" in your life. The next time someone treats you in a way you don't like, just say to yourself, "It would be nice if my friend didn't do that, but people don't always act the way I wish they would." If a friend doesn't show up on time, try saying, "It would be nice if she were on time, but people don't always act the way I expect them to."

Seeing things in black and white

Sometimes we see things as totally one way or totally the other. For example, when Sean lost the class election, he said to himself, "No one likes me. I'm a total failure." Sean was thinking in black and white. He didn't see the shades of gray in between. He wouldn't have been nominated in the first place if people didn't like and respect him. And losing the election did not make him a total failure as a person.

Many people with learning disabilities conclude that they aren't smart because they have problems in school. They don't give themselves credit for the things they do well.

Almost nothing in life is all one thing or all another.

Babe Ruth was a great home-run hitter, but a slow runner. No one is perfectly smart or a complete imbecile. None of us is perfectly beautiful or totally ugly.

One problem that goes along with all-or-nothing thinking is putting labels on yourself. Let's say you forgot to read the instructions on a test and then missed several questions. Rather than saying to yourself, "I made a mistake," you say, "I'm a real loser." People with learning disabilities often label themselves as "dumb" or "stupid." Instead you might say, "I have problems with reading, but I am very good in music."

Guessing what others are thinking

Alexandra was very proud of her science project. As soon as she got to class, she showed it to her teacher, Mrs. Jones. Mrs. Jones didn't seem to be interested in the project and paid little attention to Alexandra.

Alexandra thought, "She doesn't like me and she doesn't like my science project." Alexandra felt bad the rest of the day.

In reality, Mrs. Jones hadn't slept well the night before and was not feeling well. In fact, Mrs. Jones did like Alexandra very much, but the teacher didn't feel like paying attention to much of anything that day. Her inattention had nothing to do with Alexandra.

Many people make the mistake of putting themselves at the center of the world. If your teacher or someone else is in a bad mood, it's not necessarily your fault.

You can really get yourself into trouble by trying to read people's minds. For example, many people who seem "stuck-up" are really just shy. They might not say "hi" because they are uncomfortable talking to others—not because they think they're better than others. Maybe they're afraid that you won't respond.

Predicting the future

Predicting the future can also get you into trouble, especially when you assume the future will be bad: "I'll never get this book report done"; "If I get up in front of the class I'll make a fool of myself."

Daniel was told by a counselor that he had a learning disability and had to go to special classes. He thought, "My friends won't like me anymore." He was predicting the future and assuming the worst. This made him feel bad. In fact, after he started the new classes, he didn't get to see his friends as often as before, but they remained friends with him.

Mark Twain once said, "I've lived through many tragedies in my life, most of which never happened."

Reasoning with your emotions

Sometimes we think with our emotions—we believe that what we feel is what will happen. For a long time, I was very nervous about flying on airplanes. I told myself, "I'm scared to fly, so it must be dangerous." But flying is much safer than driving a car, which doesn't scare me at all.

You might tell yourself, "I hate to study, so I don't

have to." Of course you don't like to study. Who does? But it's still necessary. You might *feel* stupid, so you think you must *be* stupid. Deciding that you are dumb or unattractive or anything else because you feel that way doesn't prove that it's true, however.

Focusing on the negative

Sometimes we pick out a bad thing that happened and think about it too much. For instance, you receive many compliments about something you did at school, but your father says something mildly critical to you. You think only about his comment for days and ignore everything nice anyone says to you.

Another way of focusing on the negative rather than the positive is when you reject nice things people say by thinking the compliments don't count. If you do a good job, you tell yourself that anyone could have done it. Thinking like this makes it difficult to enjoy life and feel good about yourself.

Give yourself credit where credit is due. Learn to accept compliments and take pride in your successes.

Secrets of success

School is different from the adult world. In school you are expected to be good in every subject. To have a successful career as an adult, though, you only have to be good at what you do.

Figure out what you're good at, then work on it. If you can't think of anything, then find an activity you like to do or a subject that interests you and learn as much about it as you can. It doesn't have to be an idea for a career; just something you like. For instance, you could become an expert on volcanoes, insects, telling jokes, comic books, photography, or baseball cards. Other areas you can learn about and excel in include sports, art, music, building things, computers, and getting along with others.

Chris had terrible difficulties in school. He was a very poor reader. He did manage to graduate, and then he got a job with a construction company. He had always been good at building things and at getting along with people. He was promoted to foreman and eventually was asked to become a part owner in the company. Today he is a successful business leader.

John is another success story. He had learning disabilities, but he discovered in home economics class that he loved to cook. He began to cook for his family and friends and became very good at it. Now he is doing well as a student in a famous cooking school. He hopes to become a restaurant chef.

Many famous people had problems in school but went on to succeed in their careers by focusing on their strengths. When David Lean was a student in England, his teachers said he had "no particular aptitude for anything." He studied motion pictures and became a famous director of movies such as *The Bridge on the River Kwai, Dr. Zhivago,* and *Lawrence of Arabia.*

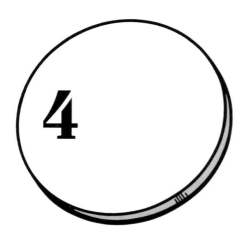

Coping with Learning Disabilities

After your learning disabilities are identified, your school is required to give you some extra help. Usually this involves going to a special class for part or all of the school day. The teachers in these classes have been trained to teach learning-disabled students. You might be transferred back to regular classes as your schoolwork improves.

Most teachers use two strategies with learning-disabled students. They try to improve your weaknesses —this is called **remediation**—and they try to figure out ways around your weaknesses—this is called **compensation.**

Remediation

Larry Bird, the famous former basketball star of the Boston Celtics, used to get up before school and shoot baskets for hours. It helped him excel in his sport. The idea of remediation is that practice makes perfect. If you're not very good at something, you just keep practicing it until you become better.

Let's say you're not a very good reader. The fact is, the more you read, the better you will become. You may have to push yourself to get started. One trick is to find things you like to read, not just school assignments. Another is to read things that are on your reading level or just a little above it. If you can't understand a book, ask your parents to help you find one with a lower reading level. As you read, you will improve.

If you have sloppy handwriting, your teacher might ask you to practice your letters so that others can understand what you write. You might have to write them very slowly at first.

When you feel overwhelmed by a project, try breaking it into steps. Jonathan learned a trick that helped him get good grades on science projects. He made a list of everything he had to do to complete the project. First he picked a topic that was interesting to him, then he made a list of what he needed to do: "get parents to buy poster board"; "paint objects"; "paste objects on board"; "buy tape"; "make labels on the computer"; and so on. Every day he tried to do one item on his list, no matter how small. When he finished one thing on the list, he crossed it off. He felt good every time he crossed something off. Before long, the project was finished.

Compensation

This approach to teaching is to find ways around your weaknesses—to compensate for them. Your teachers will help you with this, and you may be able to come up with ways to compensate on your own.

Christopher had problems with book reports, because writing was very difficult for him. If he concentrated on what he wanted to say, his writing became very sloppy. If he concentrated on making his handwriting neat, he couldn't think of anything to say! He figured out a way to compensate for this weakness by using a tape recorder. He talked into the tape recorder as if he was telling a friend about the book. Then he played the tape back and wrote his thoughts down. That way, he didn't have to think hard and write at the same time.

Matthew was a terrible speller. But he learned to type and wrote his essays on a word processor. The computer had a spelling checker. Not only did it correct his errors on the paper, but it helped him learn the correct spelling of many words. Each time he made a mistake, the spelling checker let him know.

Eric had great difficulty remembering things he heard. For example, he just couldn't remember his phone number. He was much better with visual information, though, so he pictured his phone number in his mind on a piece of paper. This helped him remember it.

Karen was just the opposite. She had problems remembering visual information. When she had to dissect a frog in science class, she couldn't remember where all the parts were. She was better at learning things she heard than things she saw. So, instead of picturing the parts of the frog, she remembered a verbal description of where everything was. She remembered that "the esophagus is behind the trachea," or "the lungs are on each side of the heart." Saying these sentences to herself helped her learn.

Sarah had very poor handwriting, and she figured out two ways to get around her disability. First, since her printing was better than her cursive writing, she printed everything. Second, she learned to use a word processor and typed many of her reports.

Strategies for different types of learning problems

Over the years, I have seen many lists of strategies for dealing with different types of learning disabilities. These lists usually promise more than they deliver. Just reading a list will not solve your problems. Nothing can replace hard work and the help of a dedicated teacher. But you might find some of these ideas helpful. Pick and choose the ones you like. You can probably come up with some good strategies on your own.

If you have Attention Deficit Hyperactivity Disorder (ADHD)

- Find a way to do something physical every day. You will be able to concentrate better if you can exercise and blow off some steam. One student with ADHD found that his grades improved after his gym class was moved to first period. After running around for an hour, he found it easier to sit still and concentrate. If you can't sit still to do your homework, go outside, get some exercise, and then come back to your work.

- Eat breakfast. It's especially helpful if you eat something with protein in it (that rules out doughnuts). Protein is in milk, meat, grains, and nuts. A good breakfast would be breakfast cereal with milk and perhaps some juice.
- Take frequent breaks. If you can't concentrate very long, work for 10 minutes at a time. Take a break for a couple of minutes, then go back to your work. Reward yourself for completing assignments by doing something nice for yourself.
- Try listening to music very softly while you study. Some people find this distracting. Others find it helps them concentrate. *Do not* use the TV in this way, though. It's just too distracting.
- Chew gum (sugarless to avoid tooth decay). It gives you something to do if your mind wanders for an instant. Then you can get back to work right away.
- Get enough sleep. When you're tired, it's very hard to concentrate.
- Get organized! This is one of the biggest problems for people with ADHD and other learning disabilities.

- Set aside a special place to do your homework. Get into a routine. Do your homework at the same place and the same time every day.
- Sit at the front of the classroom.
- Keep things off your desk, except what you are working on.
- Consider medication to help your ability to concentrate. This is something you and your parents should discuss with your doctor. (We'll talk more about medication in Chapter 5.)

Language problems

- Read a lot. If you hate reading, go to the library and find magazines or books about topics you are interested in. Look up the words you don't understand in the dictionary. If you have trouble understanding a book you check out, ask the librarian for books with a lower reading level. Try reading comic books if you find books without pictures boring. Be sure to read them, though— don't just look at the pictures.
- Make a game of learning a new word every day. Use the word in a sentence several times that day.
- Write down words you have trouble reading and say them to yourself.
- Use flash cards to remember the names of things.
- If you have trouble understanding a story, read it again. Try reading it out loud to yourself.
- Ask yourself questions about a story while you are reading it. Try to find the answers.

- Keep a daily journal. Write in it for five minutes each day. It's up to you whether you ever show it to anyone. Who knows, maybe one day you'll become a famous author!
- If you learn how to type, you can use a computer with a thesaurus to help you think of words when you write reports. A thesaurus is like a dictionary, but instead of giving the meaning of words, it lists words that are similar in meaning to the one you looked up. You can, of course, use a thesaurus in book form for the same thing.
- Follow a daily routine. Try to do your homework at the same time every day and in the same place.
- Practice telling jokes, or tell stories from TV shows and books or ones you make up.

Problems with hand coordination (fine motor problems)

- Learn to type so you can use a computer with a word processor.
- Try printing instead of writing in cursive.
- Change your pencil grip. (You may need to ask your teacher to help you with this.) Many people with fine motor problems have an awkward grip that can interfere with their writing speed.
- Use an erasable pen when you're required to use a pen.
- Dictate reports into a tape recorder, then write down what you dictated. You can buy a small

handheld recorder. You could also use it to dictate assignments to yourself in school so you don't forget them.

- Get a soft plastic or rubber device shaped like a triangle that fits over your pencil and helps you hold it properly. Teaching supply stores or learning center stores sell these.
- Write the alphabet in cursive script. Ask your parents to tell you which letters are hardest to read. See if there is another way you can write them to make them easier to read. Then practice them.
- For essay tests, see if your teacher will let you take untimed tests. Your parents or doctor might be able to write a note for you.

Problems with sequences

- Always write instructions down.
- Ask your teacher for written handouts for assignments whenever possible.
- Study the organization and memory sections that follow.
- To study for tests, outline the things you need to know, then study the outline.
- Write about your life in a journal or diary for five minutes each day.
- Keep a calendar in your room. Write important assignments and dates on it.
- Always wear a watch. Use one with a dial instead of a digital watch.

Problems with visual information

- Use graph paper to do math homework. Many people get the wrong answers on math questions because they don't line up the numbers in columns properly.
- Keep your things in special baskets or other containers so you don't lose them. Have a place for everything.
- Keep a neat desk to avoid losing your homework. Get rid of clutter.
- It's often easier to remember the location of brightly colored objects than dull ones. For example, put something large and colorful on your key ring to help you keep track of it. Get a brightly colored wallet.
- Sit at the front of the classroom so it's easier to see what's on the blackboard.
- Don't try to cram everything on one page when you do math. Use a new piece of paper if you're running out of room.
- If you have to remember what something looks like for class, try describing it in words to yourself as a way to remember it.

Organization

Organization is a problem for people with sequencing and attention problems especially. But just about everyone with learning disabilities—and many people without learning disabilities—has trouble with organization.

You may think that people are born organized. Nothing could be further from the truth. People *learn* to get organized.

Some people are disorganized because they can't remember where they put things—they are visually disorganized. Their desks are often messy. Others have problems with time. They don't budget their time well and put off doing things until the last minute. Some people are disorganized because they are easily distracted. Before they can make a mental note of a task or write it down, something else grabs their attention.

The good news is that there are some practical things you can do to get organized. Here are some suggestions:

- The most important thing you can do is to *get your notebook organized*. You can find all these things at a stationery or office-supply store.

   1. Buy the sturdiest three-ring binder you can find. Find one that has a large pocket inside on the front or back.

   2. Fill the notebook with white, lined paper. Do not get college-ruled paper; the lines are too close together.

   3. Get several three-hole dividers that fit in your binder. These folders should have pockets on each side. Use the dividers to create a section in your notebook for each subject. Keep everything having to do with each class in its own section of the notebook. A lot of people

lose class handouts because they don't have holes in them and they don't fit in the three-ring binder. You can store your handouts in the pockets of the folders.

4. Put a plastic zipper case in the pocket of the notebook. Put three or four pencils and pens inside so you'll have several in case you lose one.

5. If your notebook gets too big, make two notebooks: one for the morning and one for the afternoon.

6. Once you've finished an assignment, put it in the appropriate section of the notebook. All you have to do is remember to bring your notebook to class, and everything is taken care of.

You might want to tape your schedule of classes on the notebook, if you have trouble remembering it.

• Keep a list of important things you have to do. As you accomplish each one, draw a line through it. You can use a pocket-sized spiral notebook and keep it in the pocket in your notebook.

• Get a watch with a big dial.

• Set your clocks and watches 15 minutes early. It's better to be too early than too late.

• When taking a timed test, take off your watch and put it in front of you so you can see how much time you have left to complete the test.

Memory

Memory problems are very common among people with learning disabilities. In fact, most people would like to improve their memory. Just as with organizational skills, you can learn to improve your memory. Some experts believe that many people who appear to have a bad memory just haven't learned how to use the memory they have. Anyone can improve his or her memory. The more you practice, the better you'll become.

Here are some tips that experts have found will help your memory:

- Sometimes the problem isn't remembering something, but getting to the correct part of your brain to find the information. Have you ever seen someone you knew, but couldn't think of his or her name? Have you ever remembered the answer to a question on a test just after you turned it in? The information was in your brain all the time, but you couldn't get to it when you needed it.

  To find information in your brain, you may need a key to unlock it. Have you ever heard an old song that triggered a rush of memories? The song was the key to those memories. You can use mental keys to remember things. An old-fashioned way to do this is to tie a string around your finger. The string represents what you are supposed to remember. Other "keys" might be a mark on your hand or a sticky-pad note placed in a prominent place.

- Another way to develop memory skills is to remember fewer things. You can't remember everything, so you must decide what is important to remember and what is not. The best way to do this is to *understand* what you're trying to remember. This is especially important for subjects such as math. It is possible to remember things without understanding them, like the parrot who talks but has no idea what it's saying. You can memorize facts without understanding them, but chances are they won't stay in your brain for long. Try to grasp the big picture and not just all the details.
- Use as many senses as you can to remember things. I always found memorizing dates really boring and difficult, so I remembered them by saying them out loud or singing them (hearing), by writing them down over and over (touch), and by looking at them (sight).
- Try breaking information into small chunks. Which is easier to remember, 3148895625, or (314) 889-5625?
- Remember items in chains. Most of us learn the alphabet as a chain, for example. If I ask you which letter comes before *u,* you might say "*p q r s t u*" to come up with the right answer. You had to recall the chain of letters to help you remember.
- Put things in categories to help you remember. If, for example, you want to remember baseball

players, you might group them in categories, such as "players with the highest batting averages," "players with the most home runs," and so on.

- Some people are able to remember long lists of things by making up ridiculous stories about them. The more bizarre the story, the better. Let's say that you have to remember the state capitals of Missouri, Arkansas, and Louisiana. They are Jefferson City, Little Rock, and Baton Rouge. You might say to yourself, there's a *city* in Missouri where everyone looks like Thomas *Jefferson*. Arkansas is full of *little rocks* that get between your toes when you walk. In Louisiana they have bats that live on red rocks. If you see one, it might be called a *bat on rouge* ("rouge" is another way to say red).

Suppose you have to remember a grocery list of oranges, apples, cereal, milk, napkins, hot dogs, buns, and mustard. You could make up a story about them. It's easy to remember hot dogs, mustard, and buns because they go together. You could think of a boy eating a *hot dog,* which is made with *hot dog buns* and *mustard.* Then he pours *milk* into a bowl of *cereal.* He accidentally dumps it on the table. He needs a *napkin* to clean it up. His mother is so mad at him for making a mess that she throws *apples* and *oranges* and hits him in the head. The more ridiculous the story, the easier it is to remember.

- Rhymes are another way to remember things. Many people remember the date Christopher Columbus arrived in America by saying "Columbus sailed the ocean blue in fourteen hundred ninety-two."
- Another trick is to make up a silly sentence in which the first letter of each word stands for something you have to remember. For example, music teachers use this trick to teach people to read music. *Every Good Boy Does Fine* is a way to remember the notes E, G, B, D, and F, which fall on the lines of the treble staff in written music. *All Cows Eat Grass* stands for A, C, E, and G, which are the notes in the spaces on the bass staff.
- You can also use acronyms. In an acronym, the first letter of a word stands for something else. To go back to our grocery list, you could remember cereal, oranges, milk, and buns by the word "comb":
  C ereal
  O ranges
  M ilk
  B uns
- If you've forgotten something, try to go back in your mind to where you last used the information. For example, say you lost your notebook. Where were you the last time you remember using it? What did you do after that? Or if you forgot your assignment, try to put yourself back in class. What were you doing or feeling when the teacher gave the assignment? Were you hungry? Were you looking at the clock waiting for class to get out?

- If you find you just can't remember something, go on to another activity. Your brain might continue to try and find the answer, like a computer making a search.
- Finally, don't expect to remember everything. If you write the really important things down, you won't have to remember them. All you have to do is remember where you wrote them.

Putting things off (procrastination)

Procrastination is a problem for most people. It's an even bigger problem if you have learning disabilities. Since students with learning disabilities find it hard to do schoolwork, they have an even harder time getting started.

Many students say to themselves, "I'll wait until I feel like it to start my homework." But if your homework is in a subject you find extremely boring, are you ever really going to feel like doing it? Probably not.

Successful people have found that they can't wait to "get in the mood" to work. Action comes first. Do not wait until you feel like starting something to start it. Once you get started on something, you'll probably get into it. And when you've made progress you will feel much better.

Another reason for putting things off is that the work just seems too hard. You might think that people who accomplish a lot did so without having to work hard—that it came easily for them. This is just not true. To accomplish anything worthwhile, you have to overcome enormous obstacles. People who succeed *expect* frustrations and obstacles. Everyone fails. Everyone gets knocked down. The people who succeed get up and try again.

Telling yourself that school should be easy is another example of "should" thinking. Yes, *it would be nice if* school were always easy. The problem is, it isn't. Few worthwhile things in life come easily.

There are some tricks to help you get started on something you don't want to do.

- Do some small part of your work first. Let's say you have to write a book report that you've been dreading. First, get your desk ready. Put the book you need on the desk. Sharpen your pencil. Tell yourself you're not going to do the whole report just yet. All you have to do is get things ready. Or you can tell yourself you're just going to read part of an assignment now, not the whole thing.

- Another reason for putting things off is the idea that the work has to be perfect. Let's go back to that book report you have to write. You think your report is not going to be any good, so you keep putting it off. Before you know it, it's time to turn it in and you haven't written a single word.

  If you lower your standards a little, you will find it easier to start. It's better to turn in a less-than-perfect book report than no report at all. Don't wait until you can think of something perfect or clever to say. Just start writing. If it doesn't look good, you can go back and change it later.

Medical Treatments

Sometimes your doctor can help you cope with school problems. He or she will do a checkup to make sure you don't have any physical problems that might affect learning, such as hearing or vision loss.

He or she may also evaluate your ability to pay attention. The doctor will collect information from you, your parents, and your teachers. If the doctor decides you have Attention Deficit Hyperactivity Disorder, he or she may prescribe a medicine to help.

Medication helps most people with attention problems—but it does not help people with learning disabilities who *do not* have attention problems. It's not good for language problems, for example. Whether or not to use medication is a difficult decision that you and your parents will need to discuss with your doctor.

There are several medicines that help people pay attention. The most common are Ritalin (also called methylphenidate) and Dexedrine. Three out of four people with ADHD are helped by one of these medicines. In about one out of four cases, however, the medicine doesn't seem to help.

Doctors aren't exactly sure how the medicines work, but they seem to correct a chemical imbalance in the brain. The medicines make it easier to concentrate, to keep your mind focused on things you have to do. They also seem to help people think about the effects of their actions before they do them. The medicines also improve handwriting.

Medication won't cure your attention problems, but it can often help you cope with them. The medicine helps while it's in your system, but when you don't take it, you're back to the way you usually are. It's a lot like wearing eyeglasses. If you don't wear them, you can't see very well. When you put them on, you see much better. The glasses don't change your eyes. They just help you cope with a vision problem.

A lot of kids get angry because they feel they shouldn't have to take medicine. But that does no more good than getting angry about wearing glasses. Anger won't help you see any better.

Several things can happen when people take medicine for ADHD. Some people are not helped at all. For others, the medicine does help. Teachers and parents notice an improvement and the students themselves can tell they're better. Some students benefit from the medicine but don't notice it themselves. Their teachers notice an improvement, and their grades improve, but the students themselves insist that the medicine isn't helping! This causes problems because they may not want to keep taking the medicine, even though it helps.

Some students notice that taking medicine doesn't help them much at home, but it helps a lot at school. You might not need to take medication at home, because you don't need to concentrate as much there. At home, you can get up when you feel like it, for example. You don't have to ask permission to go to the bathroom. You can take more frequent breaks. Many people, however, need to take medication at home as well as at school.

The effects of Ritalin (methylphenidate) usually last for three or four hours. To get through the day, you might have to take a dose at lunch. Dexedrine lasts about the same length of time. Dexedrine also comes in a timed release form that usually lasts the entire school day. You can take it at home and not have to worry about going to the nurse at school. Many students prefer it because of that. (Ritalin also comes in a timed release form, but many doctors don't think it works very well.) There are other medications for attention problems. Ask your doctor about it if you're on a different one.

You might wonder how many years you will need to take medicine. The answer is as long as you need it. Fortunately, your ability to concentrate improves as you get older. About half the kids on medicines like Ritalin can stop taking it by high school. Some adults benefit from medications for attention problems.

Treatments that don't work

Because learning disabilities can be so frustrating, doctors and teachers have come up with many ideas about how to treat them. Unfortunately, some methods that have been tried by well-meaning people do not really help. Recently a group of experts on learning disabilities got together and came up with a list of treatments that *do not* work. They include glasses with colored lenses, eye exercises, special diets, and right-left training (exercises that are supposed to keep you from being confused about whether you are left- or right-handed).

Conclusion

Having a learning disability does not make you a bad person or a stupid person. You can be very intelligent and have learning disabilities. The biggest problem most people with learning disabilities face is not the learning disability. It's the way they cope with it. Everyone has problems. Everyone gets knocked down. Everyone fails. The people who succeed are the ones who get up and try again. You may not be able to change the fact that schoolwork is hard for you. But you can always change your attitude. For most people, feeling sorry for yourself and giving up is a much bigger handicap than any learning disability.

Glossary

Attention Deficit Hyperactivity Disorder (ADHD)— a condition that affects a person's ability to concentrate

compensation—finding ways to get around, or compensate for, weaknesses

dyslexia—difficulty with reading

fine motor skills—the ability to control one's finger movements

learning disability—a condition in which someone has problems learning despite being taught well and trying hard to learn

long-term memory—the part of the brain that stores information on a permanent or long-term basis

psychologist—a doctor who treats people for problems with the mind and behavior

remediation—working to improve weaknesses by practice and repetition

sequence—a series of connected or continuous elements or steps

short-term memory—the part of the brain that stores information that needs to be remembered for only a short time

toxins—harmful or poisonous substances

visual perceptual skills—the ability to understand and interpret visual information

For Further Reading

Fisher, Gary L., and Rhoda Woods Cummings. *The Survival Guide for Kids with LD** (Learning Differences).* Minneapolis: Free Spirit, 1990.

Gilson, Jamie. *Do Bananas Chew Gum?* New York: Lothrop, Lee & Shepard, 1980.

Greenwald, Sheila. *Will the Real Gertrude Hollings Please Stand Up?* Boston: Little, Brown & Co., 1983.

Hayes, Marnell. *The Tuned-in, Turned-on Book about Learning Problems.* Novato, CA: Academic Therapy Publications, 1974.

Knox, Jean McBee. *Learning Disabilities.* New York: Chelsea House, 1989.

Levine, Mel. *Keeping a Head in School: A Student's Book about Learning Abilities and Learning Disabilities.* Cambridge, MA: Educators Publishing Service, 1990.

Pevzner, Stella. *Keep Stompin' Till the Music Stops.* New York: The Seabury Press, 1977.

Rinkoff, Barbara. *The Watchers.* New York: Alfred A. Knopf, 1972.

Resources

CHADD (Children with Attention Deficit Disorder)
499 NW 70th Avenue, Suite 308
Plantation, FL 33317
(305) 587-3700
An organization for parents of children and teenagers with ADD.

Directory of Facilities and Services for the Learning Disabled. Available from:
Academic Therapy Publications
20 Commercial Blvd.
Novato, CA 94949
(800) 422-7249

Learning Disabilities Association of America
4156 Library Road
Pittsburgh, PA 15234
(412) 341-1515
Provides information and support about learning disabilities.

National Center for Learning Disabilities (NCLD)
99 Park Avenue, 6th Floor
New York, NY 10016
(212) 687-7211
Resources and information for and about children with learning disabilities.

Orton Dyslexia Society
Chester Building, Suite 382
8600 Lasalle Road
Baltimore, MD 21286
(410) 296-0232
An organization for people with dyslexia.

Index